HOME ALONE 3

Adapted by Nancy E. Krulik

Based on the motion picture screenplay written by John Hughes

Scholastic Inc.

New York Toronto London Auckland Sydney

HOME ALONe 3

TWENTIETH CENTURY FOX PRESENTS A JOHN HUGHES PRODUCTION "HOME ALONE 3" ALEX D. LINZ HAVILAND MORRIS
MUSIC BY NICK GLENNIE-SMITH FILM EDITORS BRUCE GREEN, A.C.E. MALCOLM CAMPBELL PRODUCTION DESIGNER HENRY BUMSTEAD DIRECTOR OF PHOTOGRAPHY JULIO MACAT EXECUTIVE PRODUCER HILTON GREEN
PRODUCED BY JOHN HUGHES RICARDO MESTRES WRITTEN BY JOHN HUGHES DIRECTED BY RAJA GOSNELL
READ THE NEW HOME ALONE 3 BOOKS BY SCHOLASTIC, INC.

ISBN 0-590-94946-2

12 11 10 9 8 7 6 5 4 3 2   8 9/9 0 1 2/0

Designed by Joan Ferrigno

Printed in the U.S.A.

First Scholastic printing, December 1997

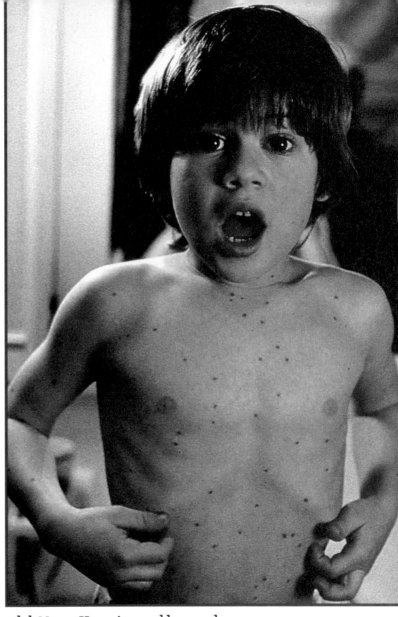

Alex Pruitt tried hard not to scratch the itchy red spots that had sprung up all over his body. *Chicken pox! What an embarrassing disease!*

Alex's day had been lousy even before he'd found he had chicken pox. He'd spent the whole morning shoveling old Mrs. Hess's walk, and she'd given him a stupid remote control car instead of money. Mrs. Hess discovered the car when she got home from vacation. She'd taken someone else's luggage by mistake, and the car was in the other person's bags. *A toy car instead of cash? What a ripoff!*

3

The next day didn't get any better. Alex's brother, Stan, and sister, Molly, spent the morning calling him names like "scar-butt." And his mom and dad argued about who would have to stay home with Alex. They both worked and neither one could be away from the office for a whole week.

Finally, Alex's mom agreed to stay home. But that afternoon, she had to leave Alex by himself. "I just have to pick up some work and sign some papers," Mrs. Pruitt assured her son. "I'll only be gone an hour."

Home alone? Alex didn't like the sound of that! "What do I do if there's a tornado?" Alex nervously asked his mother.

"They don't happen in winter," she assured him as she packed her briefcase.

"What about crooks?" Alex tried.

"I don't think that's a problem during the day," Mrs. Pruitt answered.

Alex frowned. "Nobody's home during the day. I'm only eight and I figured that out. Don't you think a crook could figure it out, too?"

But nothing Alex said could persuade his mother to stay. After she left for the office, Alex searched his room, looking for something to do. There was nothing good on TV, and there was no one to talk to—except Stan's stupid parrot. So Alex did what he usually did when he was bored—he spied on the neighbors with his telescope. Alex didn't really expect to see anything unusual.

Alex was wrong.

Through the telescope lens, Alex spotted a gray van parked outside the Steffans' house. That was odd, because no one in his neighborhood drove a gray van. Alex aimed the telescope into one of the bedrooms.

Yikes! There was a strange man inside the Steffans' house!

Alex tilted the telescope again. This time he caught a glimpse of a man in a jogging outfit at the end of an alley. He was speaking into something in his hand. A woman on the corner was doing the same thing.

There was no time to waste. Alex raced down the hallway and grabbed the telephone from his mother's nightstand. Frantically he dialed 911.

"May I have your address, please?" the police dispatcher asked.

Alex groaned. "The guy isn't in *my* house," he explained. "He's at the Steffans' house. *Their* address is 724 Washington Street." As Alex hung up the phone, he felt like a hero. He was sure he had saved the neighborhood!

Alex was wrong—again. When the police reached the Steffans' house, nobody was there. The burglar alarm had not gone off, and nothing had been stolen. The police figured Alex had been playing a prank. The criminals weren't in big trouble—Alex was.

"It *wasn't* a false alarm. There *was* a guy in the house. He had two lookouts and a driver in a gray van!" Alex insisted. But no one believed him.

The next morning, Alex's dad left for a business trip and his mother went to the bank. Alex headed straight for his telescope.

Alex moved the lens in several directions. He was looking for any unusual behavior. He found some—right outside Mrs. Hess's house. An unfamiliar mini-van was parked nearby. Mrs. Hess's car, however, was missing. Alex figured she must have gone to the store—leaving her house a perfect target for thieves.

Before long, Alex spied the woman he had seen the day before. She was jogging and wheeling a baby stroller. Alex moved the telescope until he could see inside Mrs. Hess's house. Bingo! There he was—the same man who had been inside the Steffans' house the day before!

Quickly, Alex raced for the phone. He tried to beep his mother, but there was no response. He dialed his father's beeper number, but his father didn't call back, either. Alex had no choice. Quickly, he dialed 911.

11

Alex wasn't a hero this time, either. By the time the police got to Mrs. Hess's house, the crooks were gone. And once again, nothing had been taken.

Stan and Molly teased Alex mercilessly. Even Stan's parrot called Alex a loser!

"You've pranked the cops twice. It goes on your permanent record," Stan told Alex.

"For the rest of your life, if you call for help, it won't come," Molly added.

Alex gulped. What if they were telling the truth?

Alex was going to have to take matters into his own hands. He made a map of the neighborhood. He put an X through the Steffans' house and another through Mrs. Hess's house. The crooks were following a pattern. The next house to be hit would be the Alcotts'.

Now Alex had to figure out what the crooks were looking for. What kind of burglar goes into a house and doesn't take anything?

Alex figured they were looking for something special. They were looking in everybody's house because they didn't know who had it. The question was, what was it?

13

There was only one way to find out. Alex would have to spy on the crooks when they went into the Alcotts' house. But to get the police to believe him, he would have to get proof. But how was he going to do that?

Alex's eyes fell on the remote control car Mrs. Hess had given him. The car was the answer! Alex used some tape and old wires to attach a small video camera and a transmitter to the car. Alex could make a tape of the crooks in action and watch and listen to them on the transmitter at the same time.

The next day, after his mother went to work, Alex turned on the toy car and sent it outside. He used the remote to direct the car up to the Alcotts' porch and in through the dog's door.

Alex flicked on the TV in his room. A picture of the Alcotts' kitchen appeared on the screen. It was working! Now all he had to do was wait for the crooks to get to the Alcotts' house.

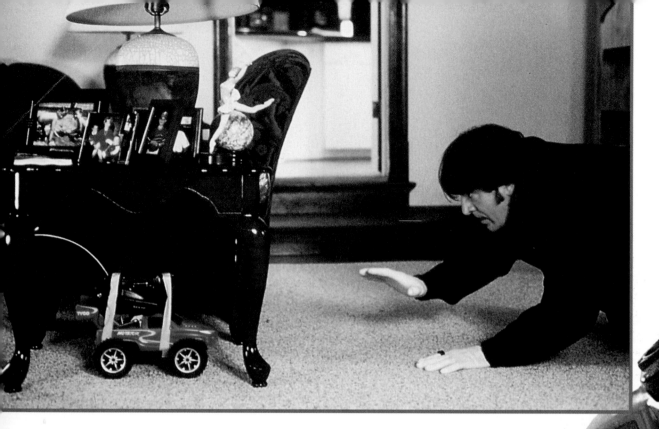

Soon the same man who had been inside the other two houses appeared on Alex's TV screen. Alex heard someone call him Beaupre. Alex used the remote to make the car follow Beaupre. At first everything went smoothly. Then Beaupre spied the car.

Alex yanked the remote control backward. The car zoomed out of the room. Beaupre was right behind it. **He really wanted that car.** In fact he wanted it so badly he didn't look where he was going and tripped over a huge basket of laundry!

That gave Alex just enough time to get the car out of the house. He pushed another button on the remote. The little car sped out into the street. Suddenly a blue van appeared out of nowhere! The driver of the van, a man named Jernigan, stopped short. He jumped out and grabbed for the toy car. He was joined by the man Alex had seen hiding in the alley the other day. His name was Unger.

Alex kept moving the car's remote control. He steered the car out of the way of the two men and into the Alcotts' backyard. Suddenly, Beaupre walked into the yard and grabbed the tiny car. The two other men ran to join him.

"That's a video camera," Jernigan said. "Somebody's onto us."

Just then a woman appeared on Alex's TV screen. He heard the men call her Alice.

"What happened?" Alice asked.

Beaupre held up the car. Alice breathed a sigh of relief as she took it from him.

"What is this? A videotape?" she asked as she tore the tape from the camera.

18

Suddenly, Alex slammed the remote control forward. Wham! The car shot into gear and slammed Alice right in the chin! She dropped the car in surprise.

19

Alex turned the car as quickly as he could. He lost the thieves and got the car back to his house. Alex looked the car over from top to bottom. "They got the tape," he thought out loud. "Why did they still chase the car? I'm sure they don't have time to play with it."

Suddenly, something fell from the bottom of the car. It looked like a computer chip. Alex picked up his magnifying glass and read the words on the chip. They said: Axus Defense Technologies/U.S. Air Force.

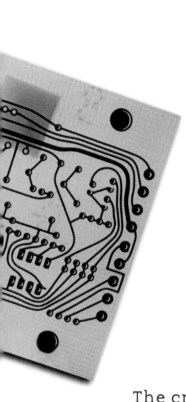

The crooks had stolen a computer chip from the U.S. Air Force. *That could only mean trouble!* The only Air Force listing in the telephone book was for a recruiting office. Alex called and told the officer on the other end about the computer chip. The officer didn't seem to believe Alex any more than the police had. But at least he promised to give the serial number on the chip to the right people at the FBI.

Alex had a bad feeling. The crooks must know who had the chip. And they weren't going to leave his neighborhood without it. After all, it wouldn't be hard to trace the car to Alex's house. It was the only one within a 200-foot radius that could see into all of the houses Beaupre had broken into.

"They're going to come after me tomorrow," Alex told himself. "And nobody will listen to me. Not my parents, or Molly, or Stan, or the police, or even the Air Force." Alex sighed. He was on his own. And tomorrow he would be home alone, again.

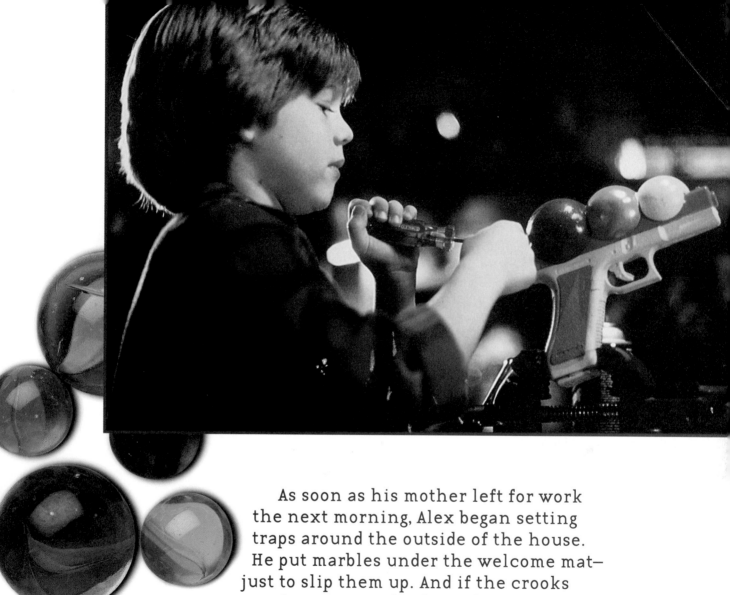

As soon as his mother left for work the next morning, Alex began setting traps around the outside of the house. He put marbles under the welcome mat—just to slip them up. And if the crooks managed to get past the front door, Alex rigged a barbell just above it. *Once they opened the door—crash!*

Alex hoped the traps would keep the bad guys from getting into the house. But in case they did get in, he'd made sure he had a few surprises waiting there for them, too.

23

Suddenly, Alex heard a loud *thud* on the front porch! **All right!** Unger had fallen for the marble trick.

"Mr. Unger, what are you doing?" Alex heard Beaupre snarl.

"Some kid must have the place booby-trapped!" Unger replied. "Watch the welcome mat." Beaupre kicked the marbles aside. "This is a clever boy," he remarked. "Let me point something out to you."

Alex watched through the peephole as Beaupre cut the string that attached the barbells to the door.

But Alex had a backup plan. As the two men looked up at the barbells, Alex released a trunk full of books from the second-story window. *CRASH!* The heavy trunk fell right on their heads.

The two crooks never knew what hit 'em!

Despite all of Alex's booby traps the thieves managed to break into the Pruitts' house. Unger walked into the living room. As he got close to the table, he noticed a pencil and picked it up. *That was a big mistake!* The pencil was part of a booby trap!

A huge bag of plaster and a water balloon fell right on Unger's head. Unger was very angry. "I'm coming for you, shorty!" he bellowed through the house. "I'm coming to pay you back for all the misery you caused me!"

Alex scrambled into the dumbwaiter elevator that ran from the attic to the basement. When he reached the basement, Alex removed the floor from the dumbwaiter—just in case one of the bad guys wanted to try the same thing. Then Alex climbed out the basement window.

Alex looked up and spotted Unger, Jernigan, and Alice staring at him through the attic window. Alex smiled and held up the computer chip. "Recognize this?" he asked.

"How'd he get outside?" Unger asked the others. The three crooks looked out the attic window. They could see a trampoline sitting in the yard. Alice figured Alex must have jumped out the window and landed on the trampoline. She told Jernigan and Unger to do the same.

"If a toddler can do it, you can do it," she insisted. "I'll cover you from here."

Nervously, Unger and Jernigan leaped from the window. But they didn't land on the trampoline. Alex had placed it over the family pool! They went right through it and landed in the freezing water of the Pruitts' pool!

28

Just then Alice heard the dumbwaiter come back up to the attic. "So that was how the kid escaped," she thought.

Quickly, Alice climbed into the dumbwaiter. *Oops!* Alice didn't know the dumbwaiter had no floor.

"Aaaahhhhh!" Alice's screams filled the house as she fell to the basement.

29

Even with Unger and Jernigan frozen in the pool, and Alice trapped in the basement, Alex was still not safe. Beaupre was out there somewhere. And he was probably pretty angry about his scheme going haywire!

Cautiously, Alex made his way to the front porch. He was shocked at what he found there.

Police cars surrounded the house. Alex's mother stepped out of a car, accompanied by two FBI agents. *All right!* The Air Force recruiter had kept his word and called the FBI. *Finally! Someone had actually believed Alex.*

Alex pulled the computer chip out of his pocket and gave it to one of the agents.

"Here's the chip," Alex told him. "There are two guys in the pool and a lady in our basement. But the other guy is gone."

Not for long.

"EMERGENCY! CALLING ALL CARS! INTRUDER!" a voice cried from the backyard.

The police raced to the backyard and discovered Beaupre being held prisoner in a snow fort by. . . Stan's parrot! The bird had gotten loose and found the stranger in the yard. Luckily, he'd screeched just the right words.

Alex was finally a hero! His mother kissed him on the cheek. His father called to tell him how proud he was. Even Stan and Molly were impressed.

As for the crooks, they got a lot more than they bargained for. They not only got to go to jail—they also came down with some terrible cases of chicken pox!